Inside a Zoo in the City

A Rebus Read-Along Story

by Alyssa Satin Capucilli
Illustrated by Tedd Arnold

SCHOLASTIC INC.
New York Toronto London Auckland Sydney
Mexico City New Delhi Hong Kong

ISBN: 0-590-99715-7

Library of Congress Cataloging-in-Publication Data

Capucilli, Alyssa.
Inside a zoo in the city ; a rebus read-along story / by Alyssa Satin Capucilli ; illustrated by Tedd Arnold.
p. cm.
"Cartwheel Books."
Summary: A cumulative rhyme featuring rebuses, in which a parrot, a tiger, a lion, a peacock, and other inhabitants of a city zoo wake up and startle each other.
ISBN 0-590-99715-7 (hardcover)
1. Rebuses. [1. Zoo Animals—Fiction. 2. Rebuses. 3. Stories in rhyme.] I. Arnold, Tedd, ill. II. Title.
PZ8.3.C1935 Iu 2000
[E]—dc21 99-046235

10 9 8 7 6 5 4 3 2 1 00 01 02 03 04 05

Printed in Mexico 49
First printing, October 2000

For Robert and Rebecca Joseph
—A.S.C.

For Nathan
—T. A.

Here is a zoo in the city.

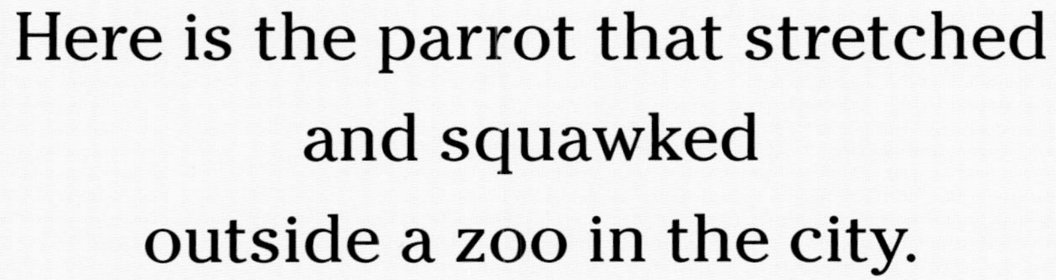

Here is the parrot that stretched
and squawked
outside a zoo in the city.

Here is the  that stretched
and squawked

that woke up the tiger that
growled and stalked
outside a zoo in the city.

Here is the that stretched
and squawked
that woke up the that
growled and stalked

that woke up the lion
starting to roar
outside a zoo in the city.

Here is the [parrot] that stretched
and squawked
that woke up the [tiger] that
growled and stalked
that woke up the [lion]
starting to roar

that woke up the peacock
who paraded next door
outside a zoo in the city.
BUS SCHEDULE

Here is the that stretched
and squawked
that woke up the that
growled and stalked
that woke up the
starting to roar
that woke up the who
paraded next door

that woke up the zebra
beginning to bray
outside a zoo in the city.

Here is the that stretched
and squawked
that woke up the that
growled and stalked
that woke up the
starting to roar
that woke up the who
paraded next door
that woke up the
beginning to bray

that woke up the monkeys
who chattered away
outside a zoo in the city.

Here is the that stretched
and squawked
that woke up the that
growled and stalked
that woke up the
starting to roar
that woke up the who
paraded next door
that woke up the
beginning to bray
that woke up the
who chattered away

that woke up the seal that
barked and cavorted
outside a zoo in the city.
STOCK MARKET NEWS

Here is the that stretched
and squawked
that woke up the that
growled and stalked
that woke up the
starting to roar
that woke up the who
paraded next door
that woke up the
beginning to bray
that woke up the
who chattered away
that woke up the that
barked and cavorted

that woke up the elephant
whose huge trunk snorted
outside a zoo in the city.

Here is the that stretched
and squawked
that woke up the that
growled and stalked
that woke up the
starting to roar
that woke up the who
paraded next door
that woke up the
beginning to bray
that woke up the
who chattered away
that woke up the that
barked and cavorted
that woke up the
whose huge trunk snorted

and woke up the zookeeper,
by jingling her keys.

She opened the gates and said,
“Come right in, please!”. . .

ZOO
NOW
OPEN

inside a zoo in the city.